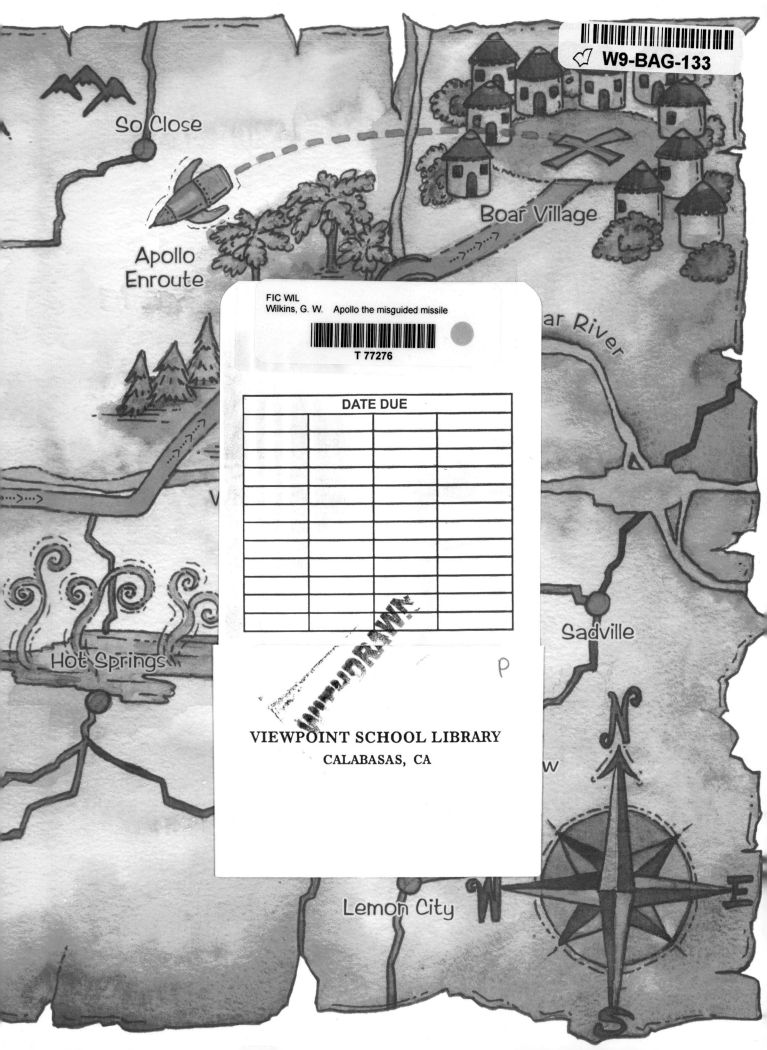

So Close

Apollo
Enroute

Boar Village

Boar River

Hot Springs

Sadville

Lemon City

DEDICATION

To my four beautiful children,

John, Gina, Tammy and Georgie.

You are my inspiration. Watching you grow

has filled my treasure chest with many

wonderful stories to tell.

ACKNOWLEDGMENTS

Thank you to Michelle Rich Williams for the wonderful illustrations,
Karen Stuth for patiently walking me through my first book, and
Sue Lion for putting the final design together.

A special thank you to the following contributors:
Dino Salvatori, Dan & Deb Gallivan, Mark & Susan Liggett, Susan Lion,
Debbie L. Cohen, Lisa and Jeff Burnham, Dolores Liggett, Cara Backman,
Ralph & Sharon Heppner, Quentin Leighty, Daniel Gallivan,
Robyn Graham-Millheim

Thank you for making *Apollo* come to life.
I could never have done this without you!

Deep in the jungle
in a land far away,
where the sun
wouldn't shine
and the sky
turned to gray,

lived a tribe many feared
who were known as the Boar.
They knew nothing of love.
They knew only of war!

They invaded each village.
They attacked night and day,
as the sky up above
would remain dark and gray.

"No one can
stop us;
we'll rule
every land.
The people
will give us each
thing we demand!"

Then one day as their leader, King Grump took a tally
of all they had conquered from the hills to the valley.

He looked at the map,
then he snorted a groan
when he noticed a town

that the Boar did not own!

He called in his general.
"We've not reached our goal!
How come there's a village not in our control?"

The general grunted
as he started to speak.
*"We're trying, Your Highness,
with new plans every week."*

*"We have planned in the spring,
we have planned in the fall,
but we can't reach that village.*
It's behind a large wall!"

"I don't want excuses,"
King Grump then replied.
"For I must have that village.
I don't care how you've tried!"

"Those people must learn
that I rule every town.
As the king I declare
that wall must come down!"

The king called his builders and he shouted to all,
"Go build me a missile
to destroy that stone wall!"

They named it

Apollo

It was shiny and tall,

and King Grump was now certain

that the town would soon fall.

In the Village of Bliss
where kids laughed and played,
the people knew nothing
of the plans that were made.

Their wall kept them safe
so they knew not of war
or the anger that lurked
in the tribe called the Boar.

But news soon arrived by a parrot who spoke,
"The Boar are for real and their missile's no joke!"

"A meeting is needed.

Sound the bells,
beat the drum!

You must soon prepare
for what is to come!"

The mayor was first to bring forth his view.
"We'll strengthen the wall, **that's** the thing we should do!"

"No, that's NOT the answer,"
Elder Elwood replied.
"They will still smash the wall.
They will still get inside."

"Yes, Elwood's correct."
"No, the mayor is right."
It seemed no one agreed
as they met through the night.

HA!

HA!

HA!

"Well, I have a thought,"
said a girl they called Grace.
"Let's talk to the missile,"
and they L A U G H E D
in her face.

HA!

HA!

"Missiles aren't people,
they don't understand!"
And they argued for hours,
yet **nothing** was planned.

Then Iggy stood up as the morning grew light.
He said he believed that young Grace could be right.
"Grace has a point! The missile might hear!
Since there's no other plan, **I guess I'll volunteer!**"

"But the tribe they call Boar may discover you're there,"
said Elmer the Wise who told Iggy...

"I'll be very careful," young Iggy replied.

"If I hear soldiers coming, be assured I will hide."

Then Iggy set out to do what was planned.

If only that missile would just understand!

Four suns had risen
and four suns had set,
a journey that Iggy
would not soon forget.
He passed through the valley
and along Whisper Creek.
The days just grew longer
and Iggy grew weak.

"How much further?" he wondered.
"Will I get there today?"
"When the missile is reached,
will it hear what I say?"

whoooooo whoo whoooooo

He arrived in the jungle.
The clouds blocked the sun,
but he wouldn't turn back
'til his mission was done.

The sounds that he heard
sent chills up his spine.
*"I won't let them scare me.
Everything will be fine!"*

He traveled for hours on a path made of clay.

"I think I am close; I could reach it today."

He stayed wide awake, not a moment he slept.

He arrived at the village where the missile was kept.

Iggy moved with great caution.

He could not see the Boar.

The soldiers had left on a mission of war.

Apollo was napping.

Iggy shook him with care.

If you shake a missile,

might I say ...

"PLEASE BEWARE!"

"Excuse me, dear missile, I don't mean to pry,
but I really must know when you're scheduled to fly."

Apollo was shocked.
for you don't usually find
people talking to missiles,
so pleasant and kind.

"Well gosh, I'm not sure.
I believe Christmas Day,"
Apollo continued,
"I will be on my way."

Iggy spoke to Apollo

of wrong and of right,

of love and of peace

and that first Christmas night.

And when he was finished,

when the story was through,

Apollo the Missile

*did not know
what to do!*

"I can't hurt your people
or blow up the land.
I **won't** spoil Christmas.
I now understand!"

"I promise you, Iggy.
I promise you all,
when Christmas arrives,
**I will not
smash your wall!"**

His talk with Apollo
put a glow on his face.
The town would be saved.
He was grateful to Grace.

Iggy just smiled,
"I thank you, good sir."
Then he went home
with news that all
was *secure!*

When Christmas arrived, the king growled like a bear,

"It's time for Apollo to fly through the air!"

The Boar were all watching.
King Grump raised his hand
as he issued the order
and gave the command.

Apollo just shuddered. He was well on his way.
He remembered his promise *not* to ruin Christmas Day.
He flew near the village. It was now in his view
as he smiled and said,

"Now I know what to do!"

The people were watching. They looked to the sky.
Apollo was coming; had he told them a lie?

Iggy knew in his heart
to not lose belief.
Apollo had **promised**
he would not
bring them grief.

Then all of a sudden
in the blink of an eye,
Apollo just turned
and flew high in the sky.

He aimed at the clouds
floating over the Boar,
and opened the sky
for the

sunshine to pour!

The valley lit up with the rays from the sun,
and the Boar started singing.
It was

joyous and fun!

They no longer were angry.
It all seemed so right,
and they laid down their weapons
for they now

saw the light!

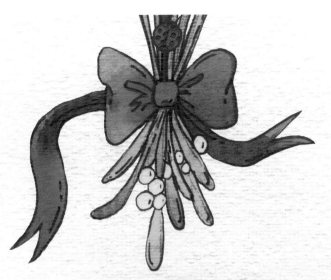

Apollo's remembered, and now you all know,
every time you are kissed underneath "missile" toe!

And so ends our story,
but please don't lose sight
that being a bully
can never be right.

Try talking with others
and hear what they say,
for hurting each other
is never the way!

Apollo the Misguided Missile
DISCUSSION PAGE

1. Why were the people of the Village of Bliss so worried about the Boar and Apollo?

2. Why do you think the Boar were so angry?

3. Do you think King Grump was a good king?

4. Why do you feel the townspeople laughed at Grace's idea to speak with Apollo?

5. Is making fun of another person a form of bullying?

6. What do you think they should have done instead of laughing at Grace?

7. Do you think the mayor of the Village of Bliss was a good leader?

8. Apollo was built to knock down the wall. How do you think Iggy helped to change Apollo's mind about his mission?

9. Why do you think Apollo was willing to change the mission for which he was built?

10. Do you believe the Boar kingdom become a happy place to live after the Boar laid down their weapons?

11. Who are all the bullies in this story?

12. Who are all the heroes?

For further discussion of these questions, please visit:
www.gwwilkins.com/discussionaboutApollo